POTION OF THE
TURTLE
MASTER

POTION OF THE
TURTLE
MASTER

AQUATIC ADVENTURES
IN THE OVERWORLD
BOOK FOUR

AN UNOFFICIAL
MINECRAFTERS NOVEL

MAGGIE MARKS

Sky Pony Press
New York

AQUATIC ADVENTURES IN THE OVERWORLD: POTION OF THE TURTLE MASTER.

Copyright © 2020 by Hollan Publishing, Inc.

Minecraft® is a registered trademark of Notch Development AB. The Minecraft game is copyright © Mojang AB.

All rights reserved. No part of this book may be reproduced in any manner without the express written consent of the publisher, except in the case of brief excerpts in critical reviews or articles. All inquiries should be addressed to Sky Pony Press, 307 West 36th Street, 11th Floor, New York, NY 10018.

Sky Pony Press books may be purchased in bulk at special discounts for sales promotion, corporate gifts, fund-raising, or educational purposes. Special editions can also be created to specifications. For details, contact the Special Sales Department, Sky Pony Press, 307 West 36th Street, 11th Floor, New York, NY 10018 or info@skyhorsepublishing.com.

Sky Pony® is a registered trademark of Skyhorse Publishing, Inc.®, a Delaware corporation.

Visit our website at www.skyponypress.com.

10 9 8 7 6 5 4 3 2 1

Library of Congress Cataloging-in-Publication Data is available on file.

Special thanks to Erin L. Falligant.

Cover illustration by Amanda Brack
Cover design by Brian Peterson

Paperback ISBN: 978-1-5107-5326-6
E-book ISBN: 978-1-5107-5327-3

Printed in the United States of America

TABLE OF CONTENTS

CHAPTER 1

Mason swam past the crumbling sandstone, pausing only for a moment to glance up at the castle-like ruin stretching toward the water's surface. Then, with a swift kick, he followed Luna and Asher beneath a stone arch.

He rounded a pillar and darted through the window of a roofless hut, shooting back out the window on the other side. Mason could swim this path with his eyes shut. Over the colorful coral, through the ruins of the underwater village, toward the bubble column that led up to the brilliant blue sky above.

Except today, they wouldn't go all the way up. Today, they were stopping in a remote sea cave on the edge of the village. Ms. Beacon lived in that cave, and she had ingredients Luna needed to brew her potions of water breathing, night vision, and swiftness.

Mason felt a rush of nervousness—or was it excitement? Ms. Beacon was the only other person living in the village, and the only adult for miles around.

But she was so mysterious! *Will she finally speak to me today?* he wondered. *The way she does with Luna?*

When a shadow darkened the water overhead, he flinched, his hand darting for his trident. He'd lived underwater long enough now to know that a drowned, a zombie-like mob that lived on the ocean's floor, could appear at any moment.

But it was only a sea turtle, charting its path through the water toward some unknown destination. Mason blew out a breath of relief. Then he remembered what Luna had told him about the turtles.

"It's egg-laying season," she'd said. "Turtles are swimming back to the beaches where they first hatched—back to their homes—to lay their eggs."

Home, Mason thought. *Where's my home?*

He glanced over his shoulder, toward the conduit that lit up the ocean floor. His underwater house was back there somewhere, carved out of a dirt mound and surrounded with blue glass to blend in with the sea. But he and Asher had just built that house recently. It wasn't their *first* home.

Mason was starting to forget the home he had come from—before his parents were killed in a mining accident and he and Asher had gone to live with Uncle Bart. Before they'd sailed through the rough waters that had taken Uncle Bart's life, too. Before they had met Luna and joined her in this underwater village.

Mason's first home had been made of brick and surrounded by enormous yellow flowers. What were they called?

Sunflowers, he suddenly remembered. The rare yellow flowers were nearly as tall as his father. Mason remembered running through a field of stems as they waved in the breeze, the way stalks of kelp now waved in the water around him.

Then something else was waving in front of him— Luna's hand. She cocked her head as if to say, *Where were you just now? Snap out of it! We have work to do.*

He blinked his eyes beneath his helmet and grinned. Then he followed her into the dark, winding cavern ahead.

Ms. Beacon's home was as hidden and mysterious as the old woman herself. Twists and turns led to a door leading to a smaller inner cave. When Mason swam through the doorway and closed the door behind him, a sea sponge soaked up the water at his feet.

Instantly, he felt a blast of warmth. At the far end of the room, a thin stream of lava ran down the cave wall. Redheaded Asher stood beside it, warming himself by the bubbling orange pool. Just a few feet away, Ms. Beacon leaned over her brewing stand, her long gray hair flowing down the back of her white robes.

From the back, she looked like a grandmother. Mason imagined her turning around with a warm smile, maybe even wrapping him up in a hug. But when she finally turned, she barely nodded a hello. Her features were sharp, her face lined and weathered like the boards of an old ship. Mason took a step backward and quickly looked away.

The walls of Ms. Beacon's cave were lined with potion ingredients. He studied the glass jars, which were labeled with spidery handwriting:

Slimeballs
Pufferfish
Ghast tears
Rabbit's feet
Gunpowder
Blaze powder
Dried mushrooms
Dragon's breath
Fermented spider eyes

He stared for a moment at the eyeballs, until he realized they were staring right back. *Ew.*

Luna poured a bit of gunpowder into her sack. Then she pointed at a nearby jar. "Dragon's breath," she murmured. "You know what Ms. Beacon had to do to get that, don't you?"

"Fight a dragon?" Mason joked.

Luna didn't laugh. Instead, she nodded solemnly. "That's right," she said. "Ms. Beacon fought the Ender dragon."

"No way." Mason glanced again at Ms. Beacon. She looked so frail, her hands and forearms withered with age. But Mason knew better. *She's tougher than she looks*, he reminded himself.

"Ms. Beacon went to the Nether, too," Luna said. "See the Nether wart growing?" She pointed toward an indoor garden built along one wall of the cave. Nether wart plants dotted the gray-brown dirt like little red mushrooms.

Asher overheard. "That's Nether wart?" he asked, darting toward the garden.

"Asher, wait!" Luna cried.

But Asher was already squatting low in the dirt, stroking the leaves of a tiny red plant. "What?" he asked.

"That's soul sand," Luna said, smothering a smile.

Soul sand? Mason took another look at the dirt. If Asher was squatting in soul sand from the Nether, he was probably . . . stuck.

Sure enough, Asher couldn't yank his feet from the garden. He tugged his legs, one at a time, and finally fell back into the dirt with a sigh.

"You have to move *slowly*," said Luna. "I know that's hard for you."

Mason laughed out loud. His little brother ran headfirst into any adventure. *Just like Uncle Bart used to,* Mason thought with a sad smile.

"C'mon," said Luna, holding out a hand to help Asher from the garden.

He moved in slow motion, inch by inch, until he had finally broken free. Then he shook his whole body and wiped his freckled face, trying to get rid of any soul sand that remained.

Ms. Beacon barely seemed to notice as she added two more ingredients to her bubbling potion: a hunk of dried Nether wart and a small turtle shell. Mason watched closely as the potion hissed and fizzed. Was it turning purple?

"Hey!" said Luna, as she stepped closer. "Is that potion of the turtle master?"

Ms. Beacon nodded, her gray eyes sparkling. She bottled a bit of the potion and handed it to Luna.

"Potion of the turtle master?" Mason asked. "What does it do?"

Luna held the lavender liquid up to the light of the lava stream. "It slows you down, for one thing," she said, casting a knowing look at Asher.

He scrunched up his face. "Why would you want that?"

Luna laughed. "To keep you from running headlong into a patch of soul sand."

Asher backed away, as if she were going to make him take a swig.

But questions swirled through Mason's mind. "Why *would* you want a potion that slows you down?" he asked.

Luna shook the bottle gently. "It also makes you stronger," she said. "It gives you an invisible shield if you're fighting hostile mobs. Drinking this potion is like . . ." She tapped her chin thoughtfully. "It's like having a turtle shell on your back for protection."

Mason imagined wearing a turtle shell during a fight with the drowned. Or with guardians, the fish-like mobs that lived inside ocean monuments. *Having an invisible shield might come in handy*, he decided.

Asher chewed his lip. "But if the potion slows you down, you couldn't fight," he said. "All the hostile mobs would get away!"

Mason looked at Ms. Beacon, wondering if she were listening. Would she think Asher was brave for wanting to fight? She'd fought her share of hostile mobs.

But we have, too, Mason reminded himself. He suddenly wanted Ms. Beacon to know that. "Asher's right," he said, puffing out his chest. "With potion of the turtle master, we wouldn't be able to fight!" He spoke to Luna, but he hoped Ms. Beacon would hear.

She did. Ms. Beacon looked up from her potion with a look so sharp and pointed, Mason shrank backward. Had he said something wrong?

After an awkward silence, Luna cleared her throat. "We can see that you're busy here, Ms. Beacon. We'll just take our potion ingredients and go. But could we bring you some pufferfish? I noticed you're getting low." She pointed toward the half-empty jar of dried pufferfish on the shelf.

Ms. Beacon hesitated, then nodded.

Asher sprang to life. "I'll help!" he said. "I'll get my enchanted fishing rod."

But as he took off toward the entrance to the cave, he tripped over a bucket. Fiery orange ashes poured from the bucket across the sandstone floor, straight toward a stack of potion-brewing books.

As Mason watched, one of the books began to smoke. Then flicker. Then flame.

The word caught in his throat before bursting free. "Fire!"

CHAPTER 2

Asher stomped on the book, trying to put out the flames. But it was too late. A trickle of fire ran up the wall, igniting a wooden shelf. The glass jars above began to blacken, as if the glass were melting.

Mason's eyes zeroed in on the label of one of the jars: *Gunpowder*. If that gunpowder caught fire . . . He shook his head. He didn't even want to imagine the possibility. "What do we do?" he cried to Luna.

"Potion of fire resistance!" Luna said, scanning another shelf filled with potions. "Where is it?"

She turned toward Ms. Beacon for help, but the old woman was hurrying toward the fire instead of away from it. She pushed Asher out of the way and grabbed the overturned bucket near his feet. Then she raced toward the cauldron, quick as lightning.

"Water!" Luna cried. "She's getting water. We need to help!"

Mason grabbed the first thing he could find—the glass jar filled with spider eyes. He unscrewed the lid and dumped the eyeballs on the ground, shuddering with disgust. Then he hurried toward the cauldron.

The water inside was surprisingly cool. He dunked the jar, filling it to the brim, and followed Luna and Ms. Beacon back toward the blazing shelf. As they tossed water on the flames, they fizzled and hissed.

Again and again, Mason filled the jar. But where was Asher?

He spotted his brother kneeling beside the Nether wart garden, perhaps trying to guard it from the flames. Or maybe he was stuck in the soul sand again. Mason opened his mouth to ask, just as an enormous explosion rocked the cave.

BOOM!!!

He hit the ground hard, letting go of the glass jar. He heard the glass shatter and then nothing—nothing but a loud ringing in his ears.

"Asher!" he called. He could barely hear his own voice.

The cave had filled with smoke now, and the smell of gunpowder hung heavy in the air.

Mason coughed and wiped his eyes, trying to see through the haze. Luna was standing by the shelf of potions, hurriedly packing them into her sack. Another figure was running toward the door, her white robes flowing behind her. As the door flung open, a wave of water poured in. Ms. Beacon was flooding the cave!

Mason braced himself for the impact of the water. When it came, he wobbled but didn't fall. He wiggled his arms and legs, making sure nothing was broken. Then he swam, searching for Asher and Luna.

Mason found his brother flattened against the cave wall, just above the Nether wart garden. Asher's eyes were wide. He pointed toward his feet, where tiny red plants swayed in the current of the water. The Nether wart had survived.

But will we? Mason wondered. *We need to get out of here. We need to get back to the conduit where we can breathe!*

He grabbed Asher's hand and led him out of the cave. When he felt Luna swimming beside them, Mason blew out a breath of relief, the bubbles rising upward. But they still had a long way to go to get to the conduit.

He followed Luna through the twists and turns of the larger cave. Finally, they popped out into the open sea. Mason knew exactly where to go from here—the bright light of the conduit led the way back home.

Hurry! he urged his brother, waving him forward. Mason's lungs were burning now. But if they could just get closer to the conduit, they would be okay.

Then he felt a tug on his shirt. Someone was holding him back—or some*thing*. As he whirled around, his fingers tightened on the trident strapped to his side. The last thing they needed right now was to fight a drowned. *We won't win!* he realized, his heart racing.

But it was Luna behind him. She held his shirt with one hand and a potion bottle with the other. Mason recognized the golden-yellow liquid—potion of water breathing. But instead of taking a swig, he pushed the bottle toward Asher.

After his little brother had taken a drink, Mason forced himself to swallow the fishy-tasting potion—and to savor it. Because now that Ms. Beacon's potion-brewing ingredients had been destroyed by fire, it would be hard for Luna to make more.

Ms. Beacon. Mason suddenly realized he hadn't seen her—not since she had flooded the cave to save them all. Where was she?

He started to swim back into the cave, and then he spotted her. She'd made it to safety, but instead of looking out at the open sea, she was looking back down the tunnel of the cave. Back toward her home, which was now destroyed.

When she turned slowly, Mason caught the sadness on her face. She reminded him of Asher in the days after they had lost Uncle Bart, when they thought they'd lost everything. But when Ms. Beacon saw Mason, her expression shifted. Her eyes narrowed and then caught fire.

She flicked her wrist at him as if to say, *Go on. Get out of here. And don't come back!*

As she darted away, back down the tunnel toward the remains of her home, Mason's stomach lurched.

He and Asher had finally gotten to spend time with Ms. Beacon—to see her magical potion-brewing cave. But instead of impressing her or getting to know her better, they had ruined everything!

We have to help her! Mason realized. *But how can we? How will she ever trust us again?*

CHAPTER 3

"**M**ore turtles," Asher said, tapping the glass with his fingertips. "Where are they all going?"

Mason gazed at the stream of turtles swimming past the window of the living room. "They're going back home to lay eggs," he said. "Luna told us about that, remember?"

He flashed on a memory of the first day he had met Luna. She was squatting on the beach beside Uncle Bart's wrecked ship, guiding baby turtles from their cracked eggshells toward the sea. Were any of these turtles swimming back to that beach today?

Mason suddenly felt the urge to follow them— away from the trouble he and Asher had just caused for Ms. Beacon. *Will she ever forgive us?* he wondered for the umpteenth time.

Asher sighed. "So there'll be even *more* turtles after those eggs hatch?"

"I guess so." Mason stared at the last green turtle until its webbed legs propelled it from view. "What's wrong with more turtles?"

Asher shrugged. "For one thing, they can't lead you to treasure like dolphins can."

Mason couldn't help smiling. His brother was all about finding buried treasure, and the pod of dolphins that lived nearby had led him to it once. Mason scanned the clear blue water outside the glass. Would the dolphins be back someday?

Then a more pressing thought pushed that one away. *Is Luna ever coming back?* She had gone to Ms. Beacon's cave to try to help the old woman, but that seemed like hours ago.

Mason's stomach twisted, remembering how angry Ms. Beacon had been. He began to pace, wondering how he could make things right. Then a flash of red—a red T-shirt, to be exact—caught his eye outside the window.

Luna was rounding the bright light of the conduit, her dark ponytail waving in the ocean's current. Mason saw a swirl of white behind her. Ms. Beacon was coming, too!

He rushed toward the entryway, preparing to greet them. Soon, Luna was knocking at the door, soaked from her head to the toes of her enchanted boots. Ms. Beacon stood behind her, wringing out her robes. Mason tried to meet the woman's eyes, but he couldn't.

"C-come in," he said, his voice cracking. Then he caught the shadow of worry on Luna's face. "What's wrong?"

She sighed. "Everything is destroyed," she said. "Well, almost all of the potion ingredients, anyway. Ms. Beacon's Nether wart garden survived. And there's still some dragon's breath, so we won't have to fight the Ender dragon any time soon."

Behind her, Asher's face fell, as if he were disappointed about that.

"But the pufferfish, spider eyes, glistering melon, golden carrots, mushrooms, slimeballs, sugar, gunpowder"—Luna ticked the ingredients off on her fingers—"they're all gone. And most of Ms. Beacon's potions, too, except the few bottles I managed to grab when the fire broke out."

As she started to unpack the potions on the table, Mason glanced at Ms. Beacon. She had wandered toward the window and was staring out, as if she couldn't bear to see the few remains of her potion collection.

"Splash potion of healing," Luna announced as she placed the bottle of cherry-red potion on the table. "Ms. Beacon makes that with glistering melon. Oh, and . . . here's potion of invisibility."

Asher's head whirled around. "Does that really work?" he asked, reaching for the bottle of clear liquid.

"Of course!" Luna said, sliding it just out of his reach. "All of Ms. Beacon's potions work."

Then she pulled another bottle from her sack and held it up to the light. "Last, but not least, we have potion of the turtle master."

Mason winced. When they'd talked about that potion before, he had somehow offended Ms. Beacon. This time, he changed the subject. "Can we help Ms. Beacon get more ingredients?"

When Asher's eyes lit up, Mason instantly regretted his words.

"Yes! We could fight creepers for their gunpowder," Asher said, rubbing his palms together. "And battle spiders for their eyes. Ooh, and we could go to the Nether—"

"No!" Mason held up his hand. "We're not going to the Nether. I meant that we could go with Ms. Beacon to . . ." Suddenly, he couldn't think of a single place where they could find a single potion ingredient.

"The swamp." Ms. Beacon spoke just two words, but they resonated throughout the glass room.

"The swamp?" Luna repeated. "Yes—perfect. We could find sugar cane there, and slime to brew potion of fire resistance." At the word *fire,* her eyes fell, as if she felt guilty for reminding Ms. Beacon about the fire.

"And witches!" Asher added. "Witches live at the swamp. Have you fought witches before, Ms. Beacon?"

Ms. Beacon didn't seem to have heard his question. "The swamp was my home," she said, gazing at a far corner of the room. "It was a beautiful place, with oak trees covered in vines. Lily pads floated gracefully along the surface of the water." She spoke softly, remembering out loud. "And just over the hill? Sunflowers grew, golden yellow like the sun."

Sunflowers. A trickle of excitement ran down Mason's spine. Did Asher hear the word, too? He turned toward his brother, but Asher was busy scraping dried kelp off the bottom of his shoe.

"I know the sunflower plains," Mason blurted. "That's our home! Mine and Asher's."

"Huh?" Asher scrunched up his forehead.

Luna cocked her head. "Really?" she said. "I thought you grew up on your uncle Bart's ship."

Mason shook his head. "Asher was really young when we left, but I remember. My mother used to crush the sunflowers to make yellow dye. She wove a yellow blanket for you, Asher. Do you remember that?"

His brother gave him a blank stare.

"We'll visit the sunflower plains. Then you'll remember home," Mason said.

Luna's face darkened. "We won't have time for that," she said. "We need to help Ms. Beacon collect her potion ingredients." She stood up, as if the matter were settled.

Why is she acting so weird? Mason wondered.

When Asher pumped his fist, Mason knew his brother was picturing the battles he would soon fight with slime, spiders, and even witches. But this time, Mason didn't argue or try to shut his brother down.

Because Mason had just made a decision. He shot out of his chair, as if propelled by gunpowder.

I'll help hunt for potion ingredients, he decided. *But I'm going to hunt for something else, too—our old brick house in the sunflower plains.*

Would it still be there?

Mason wasn't sure. But this was his chance to find out.

CHAPTER 4

"**I**s that our island?" Asher called from the back of the rowboat.

Mason glanced at the sandy shoreline. Sure enough, he could see the mast of Uncle Bart's wrecked ship—a bit crooked now, but still standing. Every time he saw that ship, Mason was reminded: *Uncle Bart is gone.* He swallowed the lump in his throat and looked away, back at the map in his hands.

Luna sat beside Mason, rowing the boat through the choppy waves. With each stroke she took, the map filled in a little more. Mason could see the ocean monument straight ahead, deep below the water's surface. Beyond that lay the rocky shoreline of the extreme hills. And beyond that? They would find the swamp—Ms. Beacon's home.

Mason peered over his shoulder at the old woman, who kept her eyes on the horizon. She and Luna had charted their course this morning, planning a route that would allow them to gather as many potion ingredients as possible: slime, sugar cane, and mushrooms from the swamp. Gold from the ocean monument, for Ms. Beacon's glistering melon and golden carrots. And gun powder and spider eyes from the mobs they might fight along the way.

But visiting the sunflower plains wasn't part of the plan. Luna had dismissed that idea as quickly as Mason had voiced it.

He glanced back at his brother. Asher didn't remember their home—or if he did, he was too busy searching for "treasure" to care. Even now, while Mason watched, Asher dangled dangerously over the side of the boat, trying to catch a pufferfish in his bucket.

As the round yellow fish swelled up, showing off its spikes, Mason reached back to grab his brother's T-shirt. "Careful!" he cried. "Don't touch it. Pufferfish will poison you."

"But we *need* pufferfish!" Asher said, sliding back down on his seat. "I mean, Ms. Beacon does."

Did the old woman flash Asher a rare smile? Mason thought she did—and he felt a niggle of envy.

"We can find pufferfish back home," Luna reminded him. "For now, can you just try to stay in the boat?"

"Oh, fine." Asher rested his chin in his hands and sighed.

As they passed over the ocean monument, Mason stared, wondering how many guardians lurked inside. He caught Asher looking down, too.

"I thought we were going to get gold from the monument," Asher said.

"On the way back," Mason explained. "Gold is heavy. It'll just slow us down if we get it now."

"If we get it *at all*," Luna said. "We may need to fight a few guardians before we can leave there with the gold."

Mason's eyes flickered back toward Ms. Beacon. Would she help them fight the guardians? She'd been strong enough to take down the Ender Dragon. *Battling guardians would be a piece of cake for her,* he decided.

He imagined fighting side by side with Ms. Beacon. If he fought hard, could he finally impress her? Would she even smile at him, the way she had just smiled at Asher?

Maybe, he thought. Uncle Bart was never coming back, but if Mason could only get to know Ms. Beacon better, maybe it would feel like having family again.

Maybe.

*   *   *

As the boat passed the rocky shoreline of the extreme hills, the sun sank low in the sky. A cool breeze skipped across the waves, sending goosebumps up and down Mason's arms. He rowed faster.

"Are we there yet?" asked a sleepy Asher from the back of the boat.

"Not yet," said Mason. But he noticed Ms. Beacon was sitting straight up, eagerly watching the horizon.

After another half hour of rowing, Ms. Beacon spoke from the back of the boat. "There!"

Mason followed her gaze. The shore was lined with thick trees covered in green moss. As they rowed closer, he noticed leafy vines wrapped around the tree trunks, too. *This is it!* he thought, leaning forward. This was the swamp Ms. Beacon had described, or at least, the beginnings of it.

Together, he and Luna rowed the boat into an inlet. Before they had even reached land, Mason heard a *splash*. Asher's wet head popped up from the water's surface.

"Water's fine," he said with a grin. "Come on in!"

Luna shook her head. "You couldn't even wait a few seconds?"

As soon as the boat bumped against shore, Mason threw the anchor overboard. He carefully stepped out onto the mossy shoreline, wondering if he should help Ms. Beacon, too. But she was already on the ground beside him, lifting her robes so they wouldn't drag in the mud. Then she took off, hurrying toward the line of oak trees.

"Wait!" called Luna.

But Ms. Beacon was on a mission now. All they could do was grab their backpacks and try to catch up.

As they pushed through the dense line of trees, Mason felt the temperature drop. The leaves and vines blocked out what little sun remained. The ground below felt moist, covered with moss and dotted with tiny brown mushrooms. Mason leaped sideways to avoid squishing one. "Wait, we need mushrooms for potions, right?"

"Yes!" Luna stopped running. "Good call. Let's collect as many as we can."

Mason hoped Ms. Beacon had overheard—that she knew he was the one who had first spotted the mushrooms. But she was far ahead, standing beside a thick tree trunk.

Mason crouched low until he had gathered the last mushroom in the patch. Beside him, Asher popped one in his mouth before tossing a handful into his backpack. "Ew," he said, spitting it back out. "Mushroom stew is way better than raw mushrooms."

"No kidding," Mason said. "So stop wasting them!" He zipped up his pack and hurried after Luna, who stood beside Ms. Beacon.

As he approached, Luna turned and held her finger to her lips. "Shh!" She held up her other hand to stop Asher, who looked as if he might charge straight through the trees. He skidded to a stop, sliding on a wet patch of moss.

Then Luna pointed.

Mason peered through the web of vines and leaves and saw the misty swamp—deep blue water dotted with lily pads. Tall stalks of sugar cane lined the edges. Then he saw something else. "Are those tree houses?" he whispered.

Luna shook her head and whispered back. "Witch huts."

Mason's stomach clenched as he studied the nearest hut. It stood on tall posts, rising above the swamp. A ladder extended up to a narrow deck and doorway. And just beside the door, Mason spotted a dark window. Was someone—or something—inside that window, looking back out?

He shivered. "What do we do?" he asked. Ms. Beacon had lived at the swamp. Would she know how to fight witches?

The old woman's eyes seemed to glow with anticipation. But all she said was, "We wait."

"Wait?" Asher blurted.

"Shh!" Luna hissed again.

Asher kicked at a rotting stump with his shoe. "I thought we were here to hunt for potion ingredients. What are we waiting for?"

As if in response, a shadow fell across the woods. A light rain pitter-pattered through the leaves. As the world around them darkened, it also sprang to life with sound.

Squish, squish, squish.

Mason whirled around, expecting to see Asher slopping off toward the swamp. But his brother was still beside him, his eyes wide.

Squish, squish, squish.

"What is that?" Mason whispered.

He strained to see through the veil of raindrops and vines. Shapes were forming in the darkness, great masses springing from the swamp and lurching across the shore.

Squish, squish, squish.

They were getting closer now, heading straight for the woods.

Heading straight for us! Mason realized.

He gripped his trident just as Asher let out a battle cry. "Slime!"

CHAPTER 5

Great, green blobs bounced across the swampland. *Squish, squish, squish.*

Before Mason could pull his weapon from his side, Ms. Beacon raced toward the first slime, her trident raised like a sword. She carried it like a warrior, as if she'd been fighting her whole life.

But Luna beat her to it. She pulled back her arm and sent her trident soaring through the air. It hit the giant slime with a *splat,* and a spray of smaller slimes bounced along the shore.

Ms. Beacon fought them with fury, striking again and again.

"Wait for me!" Mason heard Asher cry.

As Asher sprinted out from behind the trees, Mason stuck close to his brother's heels. Asher carried nothing but a pickaxe, but he was so fast! Before Mason could clear the trees, Asher reached Ms. Beacon and began striking the slime. Soon, tiny green globs littered the shore.

Mason raced past them toward another slime, raising his trident in the air and bracing his body for impact. But just as he reached the mob, Luna's trident struck it dead center. *Splat!*

The mob burst, splattering green slime across Mason's face. He wiped it with his hand, but he couldn't wipe off the sticky mask. "I can't see!" he cried. He swung his trident wildly side to side.

"Stop!" he heard Luna cry. "I've got this!"

He stopped fighting and staggered toward the swamp, eager to wash the slime from his eyes. He knelt beside the sugar cane and cupped a handful of water. As he splashed his face, he tried to ignore the smell of swamp water—the fishy scent of earth and decay.

With one more swipe, his face felt clean. At least he could open his eyes. When he did, he saw Asher standing proudly in the middle of a pile of slime balls. Somehow, with his tiny pickaxe, Asher had collected more than even Ms. Beacon herself.

"Wow!" Mason said, racing toward his little brother. "Nice work, Asher!"

As he squatted beside Asher to help him gather slime balls, Ms. Beacon approached, too. She laid a hand on Asher's head, the way Uncle Bart used to, and smiled. "You've done well," she said simply.

Asher's freckled cheeks turned pink. "Thanks, Ms. B," he said with a grin.

Ms. B? So he has a nickname for her now? While his brother flushed pink with pride, Mason felt green with envy. He stuffed a handful of slime balls in his sack and turned away.

No matter what he did, he couldn't seem to impress Ms. Beacon. Meanwhile, Asher could do no wrong. Mason sighed. As he trudged across the soggy shore, his feet—and spirits—sank lower with every step.

Luna joined him, her own pack heavy with slime. "We should find shelter," she said. "It's getting dark."

"This way," came Ms. Beacon's hoarse whisper from behind. "This way." She waved them back toward the trees.

Luna followed, but Asher lingered near shore. "Wait!" he piped up. "Can I collect some sugar cane first?"

"No—" Mason started to say. He didn't want Ms. Beacon to get angry.

But instead of scolding Asher, Ms. Beacon held up her hand. "Just a few stalks," she agreed.

Of course, Mason thought. *She won't scold Asher, but she would probably scold me!* He hung back, not sure whether to help Asher or to wait for Ms. Beacon to lead them to shelter. He decided to wait. He walked along the shore for a while and then stared out at the swamp, taking deep breaths to try to soothe his sour mood.

Uncle Bart had taught him that trick. "Count to ten," Uncle Bart used to say. "Count to ten before you say or do something out of anger."

One, two, three, four . . . He counted the legs of a witch hut.

Five, six, seven . . . His eyes crept up the rungs of the ladder, toward the front door, which was slowly opening.

Eight, nine . . . Two eyes glowed in the darkness.

Ten.

He heard the cackle, then the breaking of glass. Something exploded at the ground near his feet.

Mason leaped backward from the fizzy potion. Every instinct in his body told him to turn and run. He looked left and right. Had Luna heard the glass? Was Ms. Beacon coming to help?

No—they were still down shore, snipping sugar cane with Asher.

This is my chance.

Mason heard the four words in his head as clearly as if he had spoken them aloud.

This is my chance!

If he could fight the witch, maybe he could prove to Ms. Beacon that he was a real fighter. Maybe he could finally impress the old woman the way Asher had.

Mason drew his trident and took aim. He had only one shot—if he missed, he was out of luck. So he zeroed in on the witch's purple robes, wound up his arm, and released.

He could almost hear the whizz of the trident soaring through the air, high over the sugar cane. He saw the weapon miss its mark and heard the *thwack* as it struck the wall of the witch hut.

Then he heard something else.

More breaking glass.

This time, the sound surrounded him. He pressed his hands over his eardrums just as his knees gave way. Then he fell, face first, into the swamp.

CHAPTER 6

Mason felt someone tugging him out of the water. He heard Asher grunting with effort, and then someone else was on his other side. Her robes, swollen with water, drip, drip, dripped across Mason's forehead.

Ms. Beacon, he thought as his eyes drifted shut. *Did she see me fight?* He hadn't won the battle with the witch, but he had tried.

Then he heard another voice—Luna's. Her words sounded so far away, as if she were talking to him underwater. But when he felt a spray of cool liquid across his face, he knew she was using her splash potion of healing. He tasted sweet melon as it dribbled into his mouth.

Slowly, as if he were trapped in soul sand, he began to wake up. He wiggled his fingers and toes and then opened his eyelids. They felt so heavy! Two faces peered down at him in the moonlight—two worried faces.

"Are you okay?" asked Asher. His face was so close that Mason could only look at him cross-eyed.

"Can you walk?" asked Luna. "We have to get you somewhere safe!"

But where was Ms. Beacon? As Mason pushed himself to sitting and rose on wobbly legs, he saw her standing by the tree line. Her arms were crossed. Although shadows fell across her face, Mason could see her mouth was set in a firm, tight line. Was she angry?

He half walked, half stumbled across the soft ground, with Asher and Luna supporting him from either side.

As he reached Ms. Beacon, he opened his mouth to speak—to ask if she had seen him fight the witch. But before he could say a word, the woman spun around and led them through the dense trees.

Deeper and deeper into the woods they walked, not back toward the boat but in the other direction. Just as Mason was sure he couldn't take another step, they reached a clearing. A shack rested in the middle, leaning sideways, as if the slightest breeze might blow it over.

"Does someone live there?" Luna whispered into the cool night air.

Ms. Beacon nodded. "Yes," she said as she strode toward the front door. "I did, long ago."

As she pushed her way inside, Mason felt a surge of energy. What did Ms. Beacon's home look like? Would it be how she remembered it? And did she have any family there still? He hurried toward the door.

A torch flickered on inside. As Mason stepped through the doorway, his eyes scanned the shack.

A lopsided table sat in the middle of the room, along with a few rickety chairs and a weathered supply chest. Behind that, along the far wall, was an old furnace and two single beds with rumpled red blankets. In a corner of the room, Mason saw a brewing stand and cauldron. *So Ms. Beacon brewed potions even long ago,* he realized.

Then he remembered the witch. Had anyone else seen her?

He turned to ask Ms. Beacon, who was behind him now. She closed the door with a bang and locked it tight. Luna stood beside her.

"Did you see the witch? Did you see me fight?"

He spoke to Luna, but it was Ms. Beacon who responded. Her eyes had taken on that dark, stormy look—the one Mason knew far too well.

"I saw," she said, her voice sharp. She pointed her bony finger at Mason. "You were *wrong* to fight. You should fight only when you need to!"

Mason shrank backward, as if she had struck him with a sword. His legs wobbled, just as they had back at the swamp. "What?" he managed to whisper.

Luna reached out to steady him. "Sit down," she said, leading him to the table.

He hoped she would defend him, that she would remind Ms. Beacon how brave he had been to fight the witch. But she didn't.

"Ms. Beacon is right," said Luna, sounding stern. "You don't know how to fight a witch. They're really good at defending themselves. While they're throwing potions to hurt you, they're also drinking potions to heal themselves. You can't win against them!"

Asher threw his arm over Mason's shoulders. "Well, I thought you were brave," he said sweetly.

"No," said Ms. Beacon. "Mason acted too quickly. He put himself and others in danger."

Others? Mason thought. *She means Asher. She only cares about my brother. She doesn't care about me at all!*

As hot tears threatened his eyes, he squeezed them back. He started to count again, staring at the wall. *One, two, three . . .* The oak boards of the back wall had faded, but a bright painting hung dead center. His eyes zeroed in on the golden frame and the picture within: a green field, dotted with tall yellow flowers.

Sunflowers.

Mason's mouth curved into a sad smile. If only he could go home, back to the sunflower plains, just for a little while. Maybe someone there would remember his parents. *Someone kind,* he told himself. *Like Uncle Bart. Not like scary old Ms. Beacon, who has all sorts of rules about fighting—rules I don't understand!*

The thought comforted him. *If only I could go home.* But how?

Mason watched Luna pull a few wrinkly potatoes from the supply chest.

"Yuck," said Asher. "We're not eating those, are we?"

Luna nodded. "They're perfectly fine. We'll add some dried fish and kelp from my pack."

Dried this and dried that, Mason thought. When was the last time they had eaten fresh vegetables?

A memory wavered at the back of his mind, coming in and out of focus. He was holding his mother's hand as they walked through the market. Everywhere he looked, Mason could see fresh vegetables. Baskets full of orange carrots, their green stems still attached. Barrels full of potatoes. Wagons filled with plump, round pumpkins and melons.

The market! The thought struck like lightning from the night sky.

"We should go to the sunflower plains," he announced. He looked at Luna—not at Ms. Beacon, who was stoking the furnace.

Luna gave an exasperated sigh. "We already talked about that!" she said. "We're here to get potion ingredients for Ms. Beacon, remember?"

"That's why we should go to the sunflower plains," Mason repeated, holding his voice steady. He pulled the map from his backpack to show her the outline of the plains, so close now. "We'll find a village with a market, and we can get Ms. Beacon some fruits and vegetables for her golden carrots and glistering melon."

He wondered if Ms. Beacon were listening, if she would give him a grateful smile the way she had when Asher was trying to catch her some pufferfish. Then he shook the thought aside. It didn't matter anymore what

Ms. Beacon thought. What mattered was getting back to the plains.

"No," Luna said firmly. "We can find those things at a market closer to home."

"Really? Where?" Mason snapped. Frustration bubbled in his chest like hot mushroom stew.

Luna shrugged. "We already made a plan and mapped it all out. We shouldn't change our plan now."

Mason started to argue, but he knew Ms. Beacon would hear. *I don't need another scolding,* he decided. *And I don't need Luna to agree with me. If I want to go home, I will. I'll go tonight—and I'll be back tomorrow.*

But what about Asher? Mason glanced at his little brother. He expected to see Asher sorting through his slime balls on the cabin floor. Or maybe staring out the window, hoping for a hostile mob to appear so he could take it down.

But Asher was staring right back. He narrowed his eyes slightly, as if to say, *What are you thinking about? Tell me. I want in!*

Uh-oh, Mason thought. He couldn't take Asher with him to the sunflower plains just yet. Not if it meant going against Luna's wishes, and especially not if it would put his brother in danger. So he couldn't tell Asher about his plan.

Later, as the boys were lying in bed, Mason waited to hear Asher's heavy, rhythmic breathing—a sign that he was sleeping. Finally, he felt his brother's leg twitch. *He's dreaming,* Mason thought with relief. *Time to go!*

He carefully peeled back the blanket and dropped his feet onto the cold, hard floor. He waited just a moment to be sure Luna and Ms. Beacon were sleeping, too. The room was silent. He slid on his boots and grabbed his trident and backpack. With one last look over his shoulder, he quietly stepped through the cabin door.

CHAPTER 7

few steps into his journey, Mason wished he'd thought to sneak some of Luna's potions out of her pack. *At least potion of swiftness,* he thought, *so I could get to the plains more quickly. And potion of night vision.* He squinted to see through the darkness. *Yes, definitely potion of night vision.*

The moon glowed overhead, and his eyes slowly adjusted. He headed north, remembering where the sunflower plains had fallen on the map. He didn't have the map anymore; he had left it behind, in case Luna and Ms. Beacon needed it. But he used his compass to set a course due north.

With every *snap* and *crack* of the twigs beneath his feet, Mason jumped. Hostile mobs spawned at night. Any moment now, he might hear the groan of a zombie or the scuttle of a spider.

"You should fight only when you need to," Ms. Beacon had scolded.

I may need to tonight, Mason realized. He rested his fingertips lightly on his trident, just in case. Then he kept his eyes trained ahead, hoping that soon the trees would give way to open fields filled with sunflowers.

Would he know his old house, even if he saw it? He tried to picture it again—brick, with a front porch and a wooden door. A big yard, bordering on a farmer's field. And a garden. Yes, his mother had had a garden, where she grew her own tiny watermelons. Mason could remember eating one, the sweet, sticky juice dribbling down his chin.

That memory carried him forward through the thicket of trees. Instead of tangled vines and rotted logs, he imagined sunflowers. He heard the sound of his father chopping wood, and the hiss of his mother's garden hose.

Mason stopped walking and sucked in his breath.

That was no garden hose. That was the unmistakable hiss of . . . a creeper! And it was close now.

Mason spun in a circle, trying to see. There it was—a tall green mob sliding out from behind a tree. Mason backpedaled, trying to put some distance between himself and the creeper. But it was too late.

Boom!

The blast sent Mason flat on his back, knocking the wind right out of him. While he struggled to breathe, gunpowder floated down like rain. He opened his mouth to cry for help, but nothing came out.

Finally, his chest released. He took in a shaky breath and blew it back out. Then he took another.

When his heart stopped racing, he rolled over and pushed himself up to his knees. The creeper was gone, but mounds of gunpowder remained. *Gunpowder Ms. Beacon could use for her potions,* Mason remembered.

As he scooped some into his pack, he kept checking over his shoulder. He had nearly walked straight into that creeper. What else was lurking out here in the shadows?

He quickly closed his pack and strapped it to his back. Then he drew his trident and began walking—no, running—north. If he could just clear the trees, he would be able to see. Mobs wouldn't be able to sneak up on him the way that creeper had.

Every few steps, he glanced over his shoulder. Even without potion of swiftness, nervous energy coursed through his limbs. He suddenly felt as if he could run forever.

Then it happened. He stepped out of the trees and found himself at the base of a grassy hill.

Mason leaned over to catch his breath. A glimmer of light shone up ahead. *A conduit?* he wondered. He laughed and shook his head. *No, not a conduit—not up here on dry land.* It was the sun, peeking over the hill to greet him.

In that bright light, Mason saw the silhouettes of a thousand flowers. The hill was covered with them! He raced upward, barely feeling the weight of the pack on his back.

The flowers were just as tall as he remembered, with round yellow faces as big as his head. He hugged a stem, careful not to break it. "I made it," he said out loud, as if speaking to an old friend. "I made it!"

He'd found the sunflower plains. But where was his house? As the world around him brightened with early morning light, he scanned the grassy valley on the other side of the hill. He spotted a cluster of tiny buildings, smoke curling from one of the chimneys. It was a village—the first he had seen in a very long time.

Mason tightened the straps on his backpack and began to walk toward the village.

Toward home, he corrected himself with a smile. He was almost there!

*   *   *

As the ground below turned from grass to gravel, Mason wound his way into town. He saw villagers bustling about in colorful robes. A farmer in brown pushed a wheelbarrow full of red beets and leafy carrots toward the center of town. A woman in green pulled a bucket from a cobblestone well. As a priest in purple passed by, he nodded at Mason, who immediately looked away.

Say something! he scolded himself. But it had been so long since he had seen adults other than Ms. Beacon or Uncle Bart. He barely remembered what to say or how to act. All he could think was, *Does anyone here know my parents?*

Mason followed the farmer toward the market, hoping to find the courage to ask. At the very least, he might be able to get some fruits and vegetables for Ms. Beacon's potions. He followed the farmer past a fisherman's ware—buckets full of fresh salmon and cod. Past a weaver's table, filled with wool blankets and other home goods. Mason paused only for a moment to admire a bright yellow rug, which reminded him of Asher's baby blanket. *Asher doesn't remember,* Mason thought, *but I do.*

As he let his gaze drift across the crowd, he noticed more patches of yellow, dotting the market like flowers in a field. Villagers wore bright yellow vests. Plants grew in glazed yellow pots. Even a tamed wolf, who trotted obediently after her master, wore a golden yellow collar.

The bursts of color gave Mason the courage to open his mouth and speak to the farmer, who had paused to set up shop. "Um, excuse m-me," Mason stammered. "May I have a few carrots?"

As soon as the words left his mouth, he realized he didn't have anything to trade for them. He rummaged around in his backpack, as if a few emeralds would suddenly appear. Instead, he came up with a handful of gunpowder.

The farmer stroked his chin. "I'll take a scoop of gunpowder," he said. "For a bundle of carrots."

Mason felt a wave of relief. He poured the gunpowder into the bowl the farmer offered to him, and took the carrots. As he started to turn away, Mason pushed himself to speak again. "Do you have any watermelon?"

The farmer shook his head. "Not yet, son. It's too early in the season. Check back next month."

Next month? Mason swallowed his disappointment. Then he remembered why he had really come to the village—not for watermelon, but to find his first home. "I won't be here next month," he told the farmer. "I'm only visiting my . . ." *My what?* he wondered. *My parents are gone. And my home may be gone by now, too.*

He tried again. "I'm looking for a house that used to be owned by Mr. and Mrs. Gunderson."

The farmer gazed upward, as if searching his memory banks. "Yes, I remember them," he said. "Nice couple. They had two little boys."

Mason blew out his breath. "Yes," he said, trying to stay calm. "They did. Can you point me in the direction of their house—I mean, the house they used to live in?"

The farmer nodded. "It's close. Just take the road out of town," he said, pointing. "You'll pass a farmhouse and a wide, open field. It'll be the next house on the left."

Mason's pulse quickened. "Thank you, sir. And, um, thank you for the carrots." He shoved the carrots into his backpack and turned away, wishing he had a pair of Elytra wings and could fly the short distance between here and his home.

He was so close now; he could feel it. Would he recognize his house? What would he find there? Memories of the past? Neighbors who had been friends of his parents?

He quickly passed the library and the butcher shop. As the houses thinned out, a long dirt road stretched out before him. Mason craned his neck to see what lay ahead, hoping to see something familiar. How many times had he walked this road with his parents? He couldn't remember—he'd been so young.

He could see the barn now, the farm he would pass just before reaching his house. Crops stretched out before it, tidy plants marching in long, straight rows. From a pen somewhere beyond, a cow mooed a greeting.

As Mason hurried along the edge of the field, he nearly tripped over a patch of vines. "Someone forgot to weed," he mumbled. He untangled a leafy vine from his foot, feeling as if he were back in the dense forest surrounding the swamp.

The swamp. His stomach clutched, thinking of Luna and Ms. Beacon waking up this morning without him. Were they angry? Then he spotted something growing from the "weeds" at his feet. A watermelon!

The round green ball was the size of a cocoa pod. *Is it big enough for Ms. Beacon to use in her potions?* Mason wondered. *Maybe.*

He crouched low to snap the watermelon from the vine. That's when he heard the rustle of grass nearby. Someone burst out, barreling straight toward Mason.

CHAPTER 8

Before Mason could draw his weapon, a boy knocked him off his feet—then began to laugh. *Asher?*

Mason pushed his brother off and sat up straight, doing a double take. "What are you doing here?" he cried. "How did you find me?"

Asher shrugged as he pulled a piece of grass from his hair. "I followed you."

"You did not. You were sleeping when I left!"

Asher smirked. "I *pretended* to be sleeping. I knew you were going somewhere, and I didn't want to be left behind."

Mason shook his head, thinking about the long, dangerous journey he had taken from the swamp— through the woods, past the exploding creeper, over the hill of sunflowers, and down into the village. "Why didn't I see you?" he asked.

Asher rummaged around in his pack and pulled out

a potion bottle. "I had a secret weapon," he announced proudly. "Potion of invisibility."

Mason sucked in his breath. "Ms. Beacon's potion? Asher, how could you? She and Luna are probably already mad at us for sneaking off. When they find out you used up that potion—the only potion of invisibility that survived the fire—they'll be *really* mad." He pictured the storm clouds rolling across Ms. Beacon's face and felt his pulse quicken.

Asher stared at the clear potion sloshing around near the bottom of the bottle. Then he shrugged. "There's still some left. Besides, we'll bring lots of potion ingredients back with us."

Mason suddenly remembered the watermelon at his feet. "Speaking of potion ingredients, help me snap the melon off this vine. The sooner we get back to the swamp, the better." He didn't tell Asher yet that he had almost found their home. *I'll show him instead,* he decided.

With Asher's help, Mason slid the watermelon into his backpack, feeling its weight on his shoulders. "C'mon," he said. "Follow me."

As they passed the farm, Mason spotted a farmer milking a cow. The man waved at the boys, and this time, Mason waved back.

Then he saw it—a tiny brick house on the other side of a field dotted with sunflowers. It was smaller than he remembered, and even from a distance, he could see the windows were boarded up. "Do you know where we are?" he asked his brother. "Do you recognize that house?"

Asher blinked. "No."

Mason shook off his disappointment. "Let's get closer," he said, "and then maybe you will."

But as they reached the edge of the overgrown yard, Asher shook his head. "I've never seen this house before."

"Yes, you have!" Mason said, throwing out his arms. "We lived here. This was our house, with Mom and Dad. See that window there? That was our bedroom. Let's see if we can go inside."

As he stepped onto the dilapidated porch, he held his breath, hoping his feet wouldn't break through. "Be careful," he called to Asher. "Step only where I'm stepping."

When Mason reached the door, he tried the handle. It wouldn't budge. Then he noticed the oak planks nailed across the door at the very top and bottom. Someone might as well have hung a "Keep Out" sign. "We can't get in," he said, his hopes sinking.

"Let's try the windows," Asher said as he hopped off the porch and disappeared around the corner.

But every window had been boarded shut. As Mason stood beneath the bedroom window, he noticed a crack in the boards. Could he peek through? He searched for a log or a box—something he could stand on to get a better look. A rusty bucket lay half buried in the dirt where the garden had once grown. Mason dug it out and placed it below the window, pulling himself up by the windowsill.

As he peered through the crack, he waited for his eyes to adjust. At first, he saw only shadows. Then he made out the shape of a bed. *My bed?* he wondered. It had been stripped of its mattress and blanket, and turned carelessly on its side.

Beyond the bed, Mason could see a crib with a broken rail. Asher's crib. He had been just a toddler when they lived here. *No wonder he can't remember!* thought Mason.

He squeezed his eyes shut. He'd seen enough— enough to know that nothing remained of the home he'd once known.

As he jumped off the bucket, Asher began to step up. "No," said Mason. "Don't bother. There's nothing inside."

But Asher's face was already pressed to the boards. "I can't see," he said, his voice muffled. "Wait, this board is loose." He pried it away from the window.

"Asher, be careful!" said Mason. "There are rusty nails in that thing."

Asher yanked the board away and tossed it on the ground. Then he peered through the broken shards of glass. "You're right," he said with a sigh. "There's nothing inside. This place is a dump."

Mason winced at the words. "It wasn't always," he said sadly. "You just don't remember." He suddenly felt very much alone.

Asher shrugged and hopped off the bucket. "Now what?" he asked.

Mason glanced at the sun, which had slid westward. "Now we go back to the swamp," he said wearily. But as he turned to go, something scritch-scratched against the wall behind him.

Maybe they *weren't* alone.

"Is someone there?" he asked, his voice cracking. He held his breath, listening.

Asher was already back on the bucket, ready to find the source of the noise. He leaned toward the window.

"Wait!" cried Mason. Over his brother's shoulder, he saw red eyes glowing from within the abandoned room.

Something screeched an eerie warning.

Then the spider burst out.

CHAPTER 9

As Asher toppled backward, the furry-legged mob leaped on top of him.

"No!" Mason cried, pulling his trident. As he struck the spider's body, the beast squealed. It scuttled away from Asher, its eyes trained on Mason now.

"Come and get me!" he cried, leading the spider away from his brother. "Show me what you've got!" He spat the words, suddenly furious at the mob that had attacked his brother. The mob that had been living in the house. *Our house,* Mason thought, tightening his grip on his weapon.

When the spider charged, Mason was ready. He swung his trident. *Thwack!*

The mob squealed and glowed an angry red.

Mason struck again, pushing the beast backward into the field. *Thwack, thwack, thwack!*

He chanced a look back at Asher, who was still sprawled on the ground. *Get up!* Mason willed him. *Please be okay!*

Then he took one last wild swing at the spider, barely grazing its body. Somehow, it was enough. The mob's legs buckled, and with one last horrifying screech, it fell.

Mason didn't bother to search for the drops the spider left behind. He sprinted back toward Asher, whose face had never looked so pale. "Asher!" he cried, patting his brother's face. "What's wrong? Did it bite you?"

As if in answer, Asher's eyes rolled back into his head.

Mason's heart raced. His little brother had been bitten, which meant he'd been poisoned and would need an antidote. Mason searched his memory, trying to recall what Luna had once said about treating spider bites. He didn't have her potion of healing, but there was something else he could use.

"Milk!" he shouted, remembering. "I'll get you milk. I'll be right back." He gave his brother's face one last look. "Stay with me, little brother. I'll be right back."

Then Mason began to run, faster than he knew his legs could even move. He raced through the field of sunflowers, dodging them left and right. He ran toward where he had last seen the farmer, hoping he was still there—with a bucket of milk to spare.

"Moo-OO!" The cow sounded alarmed as Mason sprinted toward its pen. But where was the farmer?

Mason searched the pen for a bucket, hoping the farmer had left it behind. There! A silver bucket shone from a corner of the pen. But as Mason reached for it, he immediately knew it was empty. That meant only one thing. He was going to have to milk the cow himself.

"Moo-OO-oo!" The cow's eyes widened. It sidled sideways, as if to say, *I know what you're thinking, and it's not going to happen.*

"Easy, buddy," said Mason, raising his hand. He crept slowly toward the cow. "My brother needs help. You'll help us, won't you?"

He crept closer and crooned until the animal stopped shifting. It stood still and began to once again chew its cud.

Now what do I do? Mason wondered. He squatted beneath the cow and reached for its teats. They felt warm to the touch, and wet. *Because the farmer just milked her!* Mason realized.

He gave a quick squeeze, hoping there would be enough milk left. Only a tiny trickle dribbled into the bucket.

Oh, no. Mason hung his head.

"Can I help you?" the farmer's voice boomed.

Mason stood so fast, he knocked over the bucket. "M-milk," he stammered. "My brother was bitten by a spider, and he needs milk!"

The farmer sprang into action. He ducked into the barn and came out with a pail so heavy with milk, it sloshed side to side. The farmer carefully dipped a glass bottle into the bucket and corked it. "Is that enough?"

Mason grabbed the bottle and began to run. "Thank you!" he called over his shoulder. He could see

Asher's lifeless shape lying in the yard. *Please be okay, please be okay* . . . Mason chanted to himself as he covered the last bit of field between himself and his little brother.

He dropped beside Asher and lifted his head. "You need to drink this," Mason said, pouring a few drops of milk into his brother's mouth. "Wake up, Asher. Drink!"

The milk dribbled sideways down Asher's face.

Mason patted him gently. "Open your eyes, Asher. I've got something to show you!" He thought fast. "I've got, um . . . buried treasure. Asher, open your eyes and see the treasure!"

Asher groaned. His eyelids fluttered and then opened, but only a crack.

"Good!" Mason said. "Drink this, and then I'll show you the treasure." He offered more milk and was relieved when Asher finally drank it.

Asher coughed and struggled to sit up. "Where . . . ?" he asked in a raspy voice.

"We're in the sunflower plains," Mason explained. "At our old house. You were bitten by a spider."

Asher shook his head. "Where . . . is the treasure?"

Uh-oh. Mason searched the ground, hoping he could find something that would interest his brother— at least keep him awake until the milk restored his health. Mason spotted something wet and slimy in the grass. He shuddered. It would have to do. "Here!" he cried. "A spider eye—just for you." As he scooped up the sticky eyeball, he nearly gagged.

Asher's face lit up. "Cool!" he said, reaching for the spider eye. He studied it as if it were a diamond or emerald, fresh out of a treasure chest.

Mason blew out a breath of relief. But as he glanced back through the broken glass of the bedroom window, he shivered, wondering what else lurked in there.

He corked the bottle of milk and tucked it into his backpack. Then he lifted the pack, feeling the weight of the watermelon inside. As he strapped it to his back, he felt like a turtle with a very heavy shell.

Mason thought for a moment about the sea turtles, swimming back home to lay eggs. *They can go home, back to their beaches. But I can't,* he thought sadly, staring at the broken-down shack that had once been his home.

He sighed and straightened up. "C'mon," he said to Asher. "Time to go. Time to go back to the swamp."

* * *

"What's wrong?" asked Asher. He looked more like himself now, with pink cheeks and a spring in his step. "Why are you walking so slow?"

Mason shrugged. "Just tired." The truth was, he couldn't help thinking about what a mess he'd made of things. He had left Luna and Ms. Beacon to find a home that didn't really exist anymore. Worse, he had put Asher in danger!

Asher paused near a patch of sunflowers. "Want to rest?"

Mason checked the sky and shook his head. "There isn't time. We have to get back to the swamp before dark, or Luna and Ms. Beacon are going to be really worried."

Asher grinned. "Not when we show them all the potion ingredients we found!"

"We didn't find *that* many," Mason said, although the melon in his backpack seemed to be growing larger and heavier with every step.

"Yes, we did!" Asher argued. "I've got a spider eye." He patted his backpack tenderly, as if carrying a pet inside. "And you have carrots, watermelon, and gunpowder. Maybe we'll fight a creeper tonight and get even more!" He studied the hillside, as if hoping a creeper would spawn at any moment.

Mason shook his head. "We should fight only when we need to," he said.

"Huh?" Asher furrowed his brow.

"We should fight only when we need to," Mason repeated. "That's what Ms. Beacon says, anyway."

Asher threw out his arms. "Well, don't we *need* to fight to get potion ingredients?"

Mason thought about that, trying to sort it out. "Maybe not—not if we already have enough." But his thoughts felt tangled, like fishing line caught in sea grass. "I don't know," he said finally. "That's what Ms. Beacon says, and she isn't here to ask about it, so . . ."

Asher suddenly stopped walking. "Um, yes, she is," he said, pointing.

Mason studied the horizon. Two figures were walking up the hill toward them—a dark-haired girl and a woman in white robes.

His stomach dropped, and he fought the urge to run the other way. Would Ms. Beacon be angry with him for sneaking off to the plains?

CHAPTER 10

As the boat rocked side to side, Mason's stomach lurched.

They'd been rowing now for half an hour, and Ms. Beacon still hadn't said a word to him. Not back on the hill, where she and Luna had found Mason and Asher. Not during the walk through the village to the harbor, where she and Luna had docked the rowboat. Not a single word.

Asher, meanwhile, babbled on about all the potion ingredients they had brought back from the sunflower plains. "Did I show you our spider eye?" he asked Luna, holding out his palm. "I wanted to fight the hairy mob, but Mason got to it first." His eyes twinkled, as if he'd just had the best adventure.

I didn't get to the spider first, Mason thought. *Actually, the spider got to Asher first.* But instead of correcting his brother, Mason just kept rowing. *The less I talk about fighting in front of Ms. Beacon, the better.*

"You already showed me the spider eye—twice," Luna said, sounding weary.

She's probably tired from scolding us, Mason thought. While Ms. Beacon had stayed silent, Luna had listed all the things that could have gone wrong when the brothers sneaked off to the plains.

Now, though, she looked like a deflated pufferfish. But as she rowed, she kept casting sideways glances at Mason.

"What?" he finally asked. "Why are you staring at me?"

She shrugged. "Did you find what you were looking for back there?" She gestured over her shoulder, back toward the sunflower plains. "Are you going back someday?" she added in a whisper.

Mason shrugged. He wouldn't be going back—not anytime soon. But he didn't feel like telling Luna that. He didn't feel like talking at all. "Let's just finish the trip," he said, staring straight ahead.

He had promised to help find potion ingredients for Ms. Beacon, and that's what he would do. They would row to the ocean monument, and he would help her gather gold for glistering melon and golden carrots. *And then I'm done,* he decided. *And Ms. Beacon never has to speak to me again.*

When it was Asher's turn to row, Mason gladly switched seats with his brother. As dusk fell, he let his eyelids droop. He couldn't remember the last time he had slept.

Soon, the rocking of the boat lulled him into a dream. He was swimming behind a parade of sea turtles, each wearing a sunflower-yellow collar. He wanted to follow them, but they were so fast! They swam through a kelp forest, darting this way and that. And no matter how hard Mason tried, he couldn't catch up.

* * *

Splash!

Mason woke with a start. "What happened?" he asked, rubbing his eyes.

"Your brother, that's what," Luna grumbled. "Asher, get back in here!" She leaned over the edge of the boat just as Asher surfaced.

"I'm okay!" he said, treading water. "It'll be easier to catch pufferfish if I'm down here in the water."

"It'll be easier to get *poisoned* by pufferfish, you mean," said Mason. "Seriously, Asher. Get back in the boat!"

He glanced at Ms. Beacon, wishing she would back him up on this. Why wasn't she ever stern with Asher? The old woman stopped rowing, but she said nothing. She stared ahead, as if charting an underwater path to the ocean monument.

"Hand me my bucket!" called Asher. "I see two pufferfish. Wait, no, I see three. Give me my bucket—quick!"

Against his better judgment, Mason dropped the bucket over the side. He saw the pufferfish, too—a whole school of them. And they saw Asher. The yellow fish instantly puffed up, their spikes extended. "Asher, get out of there!" Mason cried. "There's too many of them. Let's use our fishing rod instead."

Asher barely seemed to hear. As the pufferfish swam by, giving him a wide berth, he lunged at them. *Splat!* His bucket hit the surface of the water. As he scooped it back up, Mason heard something flopping around inside. "Got one!" Asher called. "Told ya!"

But in the next instant, he yelped in pain.

"Asher!" Mason leaned over the boat, but he didn't dive in. Instead, he grabbed the oar from Luna's hands and held it out toward his brother. "Grab on!" he called. "Hang on tight!"

Asher did, allowing Mason to pull him slowly toward the edge of the boat. When he was close enough, Mason dropped the oar and reached for Asher's arms.

By the time Asher slumped down on the seat, his face had taken on a familiar shade of pale. *Not again.*

Luna dug through her backpack, searching for a potion. But Mason moved more quickly. He tore open his pack, pushed the watermelon aside, and found the bottle of milk at the bottom. There wasn't much left. *Please let it be enough,* he thought as he forced Asher to open his mouth and drink.

As the color came back to Asher's cheeks, he laughed nervously. "Maybe you're right," he whispered. "Maybe we should just use our fishing rod. Good idea."

Mason wasn't laughing—not one bit. "First the spider, and now the pufferfish. You need to *stop* diving headfirst into danger, Asher," he said, his voice shaking. "We're out of milk now, and I won't always be there to save you!"

Asher hung his head, but Luna's face brightened. "You found milk?" she asked. "Where?"

While Mason told her about the farm near his old homestead, he noticed Ms. Beacon listening. She turned and looked directly at him. And . . . she smiled.

Am I imagining this? Mason wondered. *Did I get poisoned by a pufferfish, too?* He pinched himself, just to be sure he wasn't dreaming. When Ms. Beacon spoke, he was all ears.

"You fought the spider to save your brother," she said. "And found milk to cure him." She nodded her head appreciatively.

Mason's cheeks grew hot with pride, but when he tried to speak, he couldn't even eke out a "Thank you."

Asher did, though. He threw a wet arm around Mason's shoulders. "Thanks, bro," he said. "I owe you."

"You *do,*" said Mason, finding his voice. "So promise me you'll slow down and be safer from now on. Starting with the pufferfish." He bent low to pick up a fishing rod from the bottom of the boat and handed it to Asher.

His brother grinned and took the rod. Soon, thanks to the lure enchantment, he'd caught a bucket full of pufferfish—and hadn't been poisoned by a single one.

It was dark by the time the boat reached the ocean monument. The temperature had dropped, enough that Luna was rubbing her arms to stay warm. But

Mason basked in the glow of the moonlight and in the memory of Ms. Beacon's compliment.

She thinks fighting is okay, he told himself, *if you fight to save someone you love.*

He reached for his helmet, which was enchanted with Respiration. It was time to dive toward the monument, where guardians lurked in the shadows.

Asher would be in danger again down there. *But I'll be right beside him,* Mason thought. *I'll fight if I have to.*

CHAPTER 11

"**W**e're running low on splash potion of healing," Luna said as she held up the bottle to the moonlight. "Just enough left to handle one more of Asher's, um, *adventures*." She shot Asher a glance.

"Well, that's why we're looking for gold in the ocean monument," Mason reminded her. "So Ms. Beacon can make more glistering melon." He patted the melon at his feet and looked up at Ms. Beacon. She wasn't smiling anymore, but she wasn't scowling either. *That's progress, I guess,* he told himself.

Luna pulled the other glass bottles from her backpack. "Potions of water breathing, swiftness, and night vision. We'll have to try to make all three of them last," she said with a sigh. "Oh, and then we have this." She held up a bottle holding a bit of purple liquid.

"Potion of the turtle master?" Mason asked, remembering.

She nodded. "But I suppose you and Asher don't want any of that," she said. "Since it'll just slow you down."

Mason winced, remembering how he had tried to impress Ms. Beacon by dismissing the potion. "Sometimes slowing down is a good thing. Right, Asher?" He nudged his brother.

"Ouch! What? Oh, yeah—I mean, I guess." Asher was barely listening. He fingered the zipper on his own backpack, looking as guilty as a wolf-dog that had just chewed up its master's leather armor. But why?

Then Mason remembered: Asher was hiding the remains of a potion in his pack—potion of invisibility. Would Luna notice it was missing from her own stash?

She didn't seem to. She had already started packing up her potions. "We'll stick with potions of water breathing and night vision for now," she decided. "We'll save potion of swiftness for later, if we need it. Slow and steady wins the race, right?" She passed one of the bottles to Asher and the other to Ms. Beacon.

As Mason waited for his turn with the potions, he stared over the edge of the boat. In the light of the moon, the prismarine monument below seemed to glow. Something flitted past one of the pillars. Was it a squid? He leaned forward for a better look.

Turtles! Three or four of them were swimming past the monument. Mason expected them to keep going, straight toward the beach where Uncle Bart's ship had wrecked—the beach where they would lay their eggs. Instead, they turned and swam back toward the boat.

"They're pacing," Asher said, who had noticed the turtles too. "Just like you when you get nervous." He gave Mason a lopsided smile.

"They kind of are," Mason agreed. *But why?* As he watched, the turtles swam back and forth, back and forth, as if trapped in an invisible glass dome.

When Asher handed him the potions, Mason quickly drank, but he barely tasted the liquid. *Something's wrong down there,* he couldn't help thinking. *Something bad is going to happen.* He stood and shook out his hands, trying to shake off the uneasy feeling.

Asher jumped to his feet. "Time to go?" he asked eagerly.

Mason shot him a look. "Yes, but remember we're looking for gold, not for a battle," he said firmly. "Got it?"

Asher shrugged. "Yeah, got it."

Ms. Beacon stood too, gathering her robes. In the moonlight, Mason once again saw the smile in her eyes. Then, with a splash, the mysterious woman dove overboard.

"Let's go," said Luna, quickly following. She sat on the edge of the boat and leaned backward, dropping in headfirst.

Asher did a crazy leap from the back of the boat. Then Mason was alone. He inhaled deeply, taking his last breath of real air, and slid slowly over the edge of the boat.

His backpack felt lighter now—without the watermelon, and with the buoyancy of the water helping the pack float. The cool water cloaked him in darkness until the potion of night vision took effect.

Mason studied the underwater world. He spotted Asher up ahead, keeping pace with Ms. Beacon. Mason gave a quick kick with his feet and stroked the water until he finally caught up.

As they passed the "pacing" turtles, he felt it again—the sense that something was wrong. Goosebumps sprang up along his arms and legs. Why wouldn't the turtles swim past the monument? What was stopping them?

While Mason watched, the turtles suddenly darted toward the monument and disappeared through a window. Then he saw why.

Shadows lurked below. Eerie blue eyes glowed, staring up from the depths of the ocean floor. Then something whizzed through the water, inches away from Mason's shoulder. A trident struck the prismarine wall of the ocean monument. Mason could almost feel the impact. The trident quivered to a stop.

Then his brain caught up. The trident had been thrown by a drowned, an underwater zombie. The drowned were attacking!

Had Asher and the others seen them yet? No—they were still swimming. *Stop!* Mason wanted to call after them. But underwater, he had no voice.

He grabbed his trident, ready to fight—but he didn't pull it from its sheath. *Do we fight this time?* he wondered. *Or do we hide?* He had only a second to decide. He glanced again at the window where the sea turtles had disappeared, and found his answer. He had to lead the others into the monument—they'd be safe inside.

With a burst of speed, he shot past Asher and held up his hand to stop him. He waved to get Luna's attention, too. But Ms. Beacon was too far ahead.

Mason pointed toward the window. *Follow me!*

Asher's eyebrows shot up in confusion, but he followed. Luna trailed close behind. From the safety of the prismarine-walled room, Mason waited for Ms. Beacon to glide in too. Would she appear at any moment? Or . . . would a drowned follow them in?

He raised his trident, just in case. As a few turtles passed overhead, the water around Mason gently rippled. But nothing came through the window.

He blew out a breath and allowed his body to relax. The drowned must have sunk back down to the ocean's bottom. *But if we go back out, they'll come after us again,* he knew.

The turtles must have known it, too. They paddled in great circles around the room, sometimes slipping out the door and swimming down the hall before coming back. *How will they get back to their home beach?* Mason wondered. *Where will they lay their eggs?*

He turned toward Luna. She would know what to do—about Ms. Beacon, and about the turtles. Luna chewed her lip, as if deep in thought. Then she patted her backpack—where she kept the potion ingredients they had already gathered—and waved them down the hall.

We're going for gold, Mason realized. *We're going to get what we came here for, with or without Ms. Beacon.*

But as he followed Luna out of the room, his sense of dread returned. The drowned were outside the monument, but other hostile mobs lurked *inside.* As he turned each corner, swimming from a square prismarine room to a long narrow one lit with sea lanterns, he kept a lookout for guardians.

Luna led them deep inside the monument, where Mason knew they would find the treasure chamber. With each room they passed, Asher sped up, jockeying with Luna for the lead. Asher could sniff out treasure the way a wolf could sniff out skeleton bones. And by the look on his face, Mason knew they were getting close.

Slow down! he wanted to call to Asher. *Pay attention! Be safe!*

But Asher had taken the lead now. He rounded a corner and disappeared.

Mason pushed past Luna, desperate to keep an eye on his brother. The hall ahead was empty. Which room had Asher gone into?

Mason shot through the first doorway, scanning the room for Asher. He searched the shadowy corners on either side of a prismarine pillar and saw nothing. But as he turned to leave, something slowly glided out from behind the pillar and stared across the room with a single eye.

Mason's fingers quivered, itching to grab his trident. But if he fought, the guardian would fight back. *And I'll be putting Asher and Luna in danger,* he realized. Instead, he flattened himself against the wall, hoping the guardian hadn't yet seen him.

The hostile mob hovered, round and spiky as a pufferfish but so much larger. Mason's heart thudded in his ears. *Don't move!* he reminded himself. *Don't even breathe!*

After what felt like hours, the guardian sank slowly back to the floor of the room. Mason made his move, unfreezing his limbs and pulling himself through the doorway out into the hall.

Luna was waiting for him there. She flashed a grin and pointed through a doorway across the hall. Mason could see his brother, hovering in front of a wall of dark prismarine. The blocks formed a giant plus sign, lit by sea lanterns in all four corners.

As Mason swam into the room, he saw part of the plus sign had been chipped away, exposing something shiny beneath. He sucked in a mouthful of water.

Gold. Asher had found an entire wall of gold!

CHAPTER 12

While Asher mined the gold with his pickaxe, Mason stood guard, wishing he had an axe, too. Luna fumbled around in her backpack and pulled out her potion bottles. But they looked nearly empty. She offered one to Mason.

He waved his hand to say, *I'm good*. Between the potion of water breathing and his helmet enchanted with Respiration, he could last a while longer.

When Luna offered the potions to Asher, he quickly waved them away, too. But worry niggled at the back of Mason's mind. His brother was so crazed by the treasure he'd found, he wouldn't stop long enough to drink potions—even if he needed them.

We have to hurry, Mason thought. *We have to get out of here before Asher gets in trouble again. Before we all do.*

His mind flashed to Ms. Beacon. Why hadn't she returned? Was she in the monument somewhere? Was she in danger? He fought down the panic rising in his throat.

Ms. Beacon is strong. She can fend for herself, he decided. *Right now, I have to take care of Asher.*

Great chunks of gold littered the floor—blocks that were too big to carry. Asher whacked at them with his axe, breaking them into smaller gold ingots. Luna scooped up several ingots and loaded them into her pack. Then she held up a hand to tell Asher to stop. *We have enough,* she seemed to be saying. *It's time to go.*

Asher's face fell, but he finally lowered his axe. He scooped up a few gold bars of his own as he swam from the room. Then he gave Mason a thumbs-up and darted down the hall after Luna.

Mason wondered whether she would lead them out the nearest window, straight up to the boat. Instead, she led them back the way they had come.

The turtles were still circling the prismarine room, except now, there were more of them. As Luna swam toward the window, she hesitated and looked back at the turtles.

I'm worried about them, too, Mason wanted to say. He shrugged his shoulders. *What can we do?*

Before Luna could respond, someone appeared in the window behind her. Ms. Beacon! She pushed her way into the room, pulling her robes behind her. Then she held up a hand, as if to say, *Don't you dare swim out that window.*

A trickle of dread ran down Mason's spine. The drowned were still out there—he could see it in Ms. Beacon's eyes. *That means we're not safe,* he realized. *And the turtles aren't either.*

Ms. Beacon reached for the pickaxe in Asher's hand. She crossed the room and began to whack at the wall, pulling out turquoise blocks and letting them float to the floor.

Mason locked eyes with Luna. What was the old woman doing? Mining prismarine, at a time like this?

But soon Ms. Beacon broke free to the watery world outside the monument. As soon as she had created a window, she reached into her robes and pulled out a handful of something green.

Kelp? Mason wondered. *No, sea grass!*

Ms. Beacon waved the grass side to side, luring the closest turtle toward the window. In an instant, Mason knew what she was doing. *She's trying to show them another way,* he realized. *A safer path home.* But would the turtles follow?

When the first turtle approached the sea grass, Mason pumped his fist in the water. *Yes!* Ms. Beacon led the turtle right through the window, and a steady stream of other turtles followed. When all the turtles had left the room, Luna waved Mason and Asher out, too.

As Mason hurried out the window after his brother, he glanced down. Somewhere at the ocean's floor, the drowned still lurked. *Will the turtles get home without being attacked?* he wondered. *Will we?*

He focused his eyes straight ahead on Ms. Beacon, who led the turtle parade. As they left the prismarine monument behind, the landscape gave way to kelp fields and sloping sandstone. Soon, the turtles passed

Ms. Beacon, swimming faster and faster now that they had a straight shot toward home.

She stopped swimming. In the glow of a nearby sea lantern, she looked young—and very happy. She lifted a hand to wave goodbye to the turtles.

Then Mason saw something rise behind her.

The drowned let out an eerie growl that chilled Mason to the bone. It echoed throughout the ocean floor, sending the turtles off course. As they veered left toward the craggy opening of a sea cave, Ms. Beacon watched them go.

Turn around! Mason wanted to cry. *Watch out for the drowned!*

In the next instant, Ms. Beacon pulled her trident, ready to fight. She slashed at the drowned with her trident, only enough to knock it backward. Then she took off after the turtles, like a mother wolf protecting her pups.

But more mobs staggered up from the ocean floor. They lurched forward in their tattered brown robes, their mottled green arms reaching for prey.

Asher saw the mobs, too. He drew his pickaxe, as if he were ready to take on the whole army of drowned.

"No!" Mason cried, the word bubbling from his mouth. He looked around for Luna, hoping she could help him lure Asher away from the hostile mobs.

Luna was swimming toward the sea cave behind Ms. Beacon. Mason gestured toward her, as if to say to Asher, *Follow Luna!*

But Asher swam the other way. Mason caught a glimpse of his brother's face as he passed. Asher's jaw was clenched, his brow furrowed.

Asher was ready to fight.

CHAPTER 13

Asher reached the first drowned in a flash.

As Mason stroked the water, desperate to catch up, Asher whacked the drowned with his pickaxe. *Thwack!* The drowned grunted and staggered backward. But three more rose to take its place, moving together like the limbs of a writhing green beast.

Asher stepped forward, his axe overhead.

Stop! Mason wanted to cry. Luna and Ms. Beacon were too far away—they couldn't help. *It's just us,* he thought, his stomach squeezing. *This isn't the time to fight!*

As another drowned approached, Asher swung and struck. The drowned growled and thrashed side to side, knocking the axe from Asher's hands. It bounced along the ocean floor.

No! Mason felt a sudden surge of adrenaline. With a swift kick, he dove in front of his brother—just as the drowned lurched forward again. Mason swung his trident with every ounce of strength he could muster. *Thwack!*

When the mob stumbled and fell, Mason took another shot. *Thwack! Thwack, thwack!* He battled the beast until it lay still. Then he climbed over the steaming pile of rotten flesh and grabbed Asher's pickaxe from the ground.

More drowned crept forward, their eyes piercing the dark water. But instead of giving Asher his axe, Mason hung on to it, waving his brother upward. *We're done fighting,* he told him with a fierce look. *It's time to go.*

To Mason's relief, his brother followed. Without his weapon, Asher seemed to have lost his fight. He kicked his legs and swam straight up to safety.

But Ms. Beacon and Luna weren't there.

Mason spun around, trying to remember which way they had gone. Then he saw the jagged opening to the sea cave. When he was sure Asher was following, he took off for the dark gaping hole.

The first thing Mason saw inside the cave were the turtles, circling the water. But where were Luna and Ms. Beacon? He squeezed his eyes shut and opened them again, waiting for them to adjust to the darkness of the cave. But the potion of night vision had worn off long ago. *And the potion of water breathing will too,* he thought with a twinge of fear.

He followed the turtles in their circular swim, hoping it would lead to Luna and her bag of potions. After a lap around the cave, Mason was nearly ready to give up.

Then he saw a pair of legs dangling in the water ahead, glowing purple with the Depth Strider enchantment. Luna! He surfaced beside her, inhaling a sweet breath of fresh air.

Luna sat on a narrow ledge, examining her potions. As Mason pulled himself out of the water beside her, his shoulders shook with the effort. He laid his pack and his weapons on the ledge and then reached down to help Asher up.

Asher immediately reached for his pickaxe, shooting Mason a resentful look. "Why'd you take it?" he asked.

"Because," said Mason, "you're always looking for a fight. We didn't *need* to fight the drowned. Ms. Beacon and the turtles were already safe. But you put yourself in danger, and you put *me* in danger, too."

Asher's face fell. "Sorry," he mumbled.

"You just need to slow down and think," said Mason, choosing his words carefully. "Count to ten, like Uncle Bart taught us. Count to ten before you do something dangerous."

Asher nodded, but he wouldn't look up.

Mason glanced around. "Where's Ms. Beacon?" he asked.

Luna sighed. "She's trying to find another way out of the cave. A way for the turtles to get home safely without running into more drowned. But if she can't find one, we're going to have to *make* one."

Asher cocked his head. "Like with TNT?" he asked.

"No!" Luna said. "More like with your pickaxe. Tunneling out slowly is safer."

Asher's face fell, as if he thought he was being scolded again.

"It's like Ms. Beacon did in the monument," Mason said, catching his brother's eye. "Mining through the wall to make a back door."

Luna nodded. "Exactly."

Asher wiped his pickaxe on his shirt until it shone. "I'm ready to mine," he said.

Mason blew out a breath of relief. Finally, Asher was thinking about something other than fighting—another way to help the turtles. Mason studied the dark water below, hoping Ms. Beacon would return so they could get started. Before something else happened.

When she did, she had good news. "I've found a crevice in the wall," she said, pointing down. "We can widen it with an axe and lead the turtles through."

Asher raised his axe in the air. "I'll help!" he said.

Ms. Beacon smiled. "Good," she said. "Let's get started." She dove gracefully back underwater.

Asher started to slide off the ledge, too, until Mason reminded him to drink more potions—and to watch his back for hostile mobs. As his brother dove back into the cool water, Mason met Luna's eyes. "Will we have enough?" he asked, gesturing toward the bottles she was placing back into her pack.

She chewed her lip and slowly shook her head. "Only if nothing goes wrong," she said. "We need to mine through this wall quickly and set the turtles free. Then we need to go home and start brewing again." She stared at the last bottle in her hand—a nearly empty bottle of potion of healing. "Nothing can go wrong," she repeated, as if to herself.

Before Mason could start worrying, he slid off the ledge to go in search of Asher. There was only one axe, so he couldn't help mine. But he could stand guard to help make sure that everything went *right*.

He found Asher and Ms. Beacon working in a shallow crevice. Ms. Beacon held the axe and was mining quickly. Mason marveled again at how strong she was, even though she didn't look it. But when Asher nudged Ms. Beacon's shoulder and offered to take a turn, she let him.

As Asher mined blocks, Ms. Beacon and Mason carried them out of the tunnel and let them fall to the floor of the cave, avoiding the swimming turtles. Soon the tunnel they created sloped upward, allowing for a small pocket of air just below the roofline. Mason made sure Asher surfaced often enough to breathe in the cool, moist air. Ms. Beacon didn't seem to need it. She was mining again now, faster and faster.

As Mason carried a particularly heavy block out of the tunnel, a large turtle swam in.

No, buddy, Mason wanted to say. *Not yet. Wait till we're all done.*

But as the water between them grew still, Mason saw spikes instead of a turtle shell. And an enormous eye where the turtle head should be. This was no turtle. This was a guardian!

Mason froze.

As the guardian's eye rolled left and right, searching, Mason hovered behind the sandstone block in his hands. *It doesn't see me yet,* he realized. *If I don't move, it'll go away.*

Then another thought rolled along behind that one. *Any moment now, Asher is going to carry out a block of his own!*

Mason knew how to stay perfectly still, but would Asher? He fought the urge to glance over his shoulder—to swim back and warn his brother. Any movement would give their location away, and the guardian would strike.

Finally, *finally,* the beast drifted on.

Mason instantly dropped the block and grabbed his trident. He turned, eager to warn Asher and Ms. Beacon. But something else caught his eye—another shape at the end of the tunnel. The guardian was back!

This time, Mason kicked into action. He wound up his arm, ready to launch his trident. As the guardian swam into the tunnel, Mason let the weapon slide though his fingers.

Then he saw the dark ponytail. And four limbs instead of fins.

He wasn't about to attack a guardian.

He was about to attack Luna!

CHAPTER 14

At the last second, Mason gripped his trident—catching it instead of releasing it. His heart pounded in his ears. In a moment of panic, he had nearly attacked his friend.

As the realization washed over him, Mason flattened himself against the wall, trying to calm his racing heart. Luna swam closer, fear etched across her own face. But instead of stopping and scolding him, she swam right by toward Asher and Ms. Beacon. Then she waved them toward the water's surface.

Together, huddled beneath the roof of the cramped tunnel, Luna told them what she had seen. "Guardians!" she said. "Three or four of them. They're in the cave. We have to tunnel our way out—right now."

Asher gripped his pickaxe. "What if the guardians hurt the turtles?"

Luna shook her head. "They won't," she said. "But *we* might, if we start to fight. The lasers the guardians fire at us might hit the turtles instead. And it's so dark and cramped in here, we might end up hurting *each other*, too."

When she gave Mason a pointed look, he winced. "I'm sorry," he said. "I was moving too fast."

Asher's eyes widened. "What happened?" he asked.

Mason gave a sheepish laugh. "You're not the only one who needs to slow down and think, Asher," he said. "We all need to work on that." Suddenly, he was struck with a thought. "We all need to slow down," he repeated. "We need the potion of the turtle master. It'll protect us!"

Luna nodded, but a shadow hung over her face. "We don't have enough for the four of us."

Ms. Beacon had been studying the wall of the cave, as if mining through it in her mind. She turned. "You three take the potion," she said. "I'll be fine."

Somehow, Mason believed she would.

Luna pulled the bottle from her pack. "I think there's only enough for two," she said. She pushed the bottle toward Mason. "You and Asher," she said.

"No way!" Asher said, swimming backward. "It'll slow down our mining. That's the one thing we have to do *fast*—get out of this cave. You said so yourself!"

Luna hesitated. "You might be right."

"No," said Mason, reaching for Asher's axe. "I'll do the mining. You drink the potion and stay safe."

But Asher wouldn't give over the axe. He hung on tight, locking eyes with Mason. "It's *my* axe," he said.

Finally, Mason let go. There was no winning against Asher when he got like this. He was as tough as obsidian, just like Uncle Bart. "Fine," Mason said. "But I'm standing guard at the end of the tunnel. I won't let the guardians near you," he promised.

"Me, neither," Luna said. She took a small swig of the potion and offered it to Mason.

He sipped carefully, wondering how the purple potion would taste. *Like fish,* he decided as he recorked the bottle. But his fingers fumbled. As he passed the bottle back to Luna, he felt as if he were moving through mud or clay. "What's happening?" he asked.

Luna answered slowly, drawing out her words. "The potion is working," she said. "It's slowing us down, but don't worry. You're stronger now. You have an invisible shield—like a turtle shell, remember?"

Mason nodded ever so slowly. He drifted back underwater and inched his way toward the opening of the tunnel.

Turtles swam past, barely noticing him. Luna was beside him now, too, her limbs floating lazily in the water. *She looks like a squid,* he thought. *And I feel like one.*

As a guardian drifted into view, Mason held his breath and stayed perfectly still, allowing his body to float downward to the base of the tunnel. Staying still was easier now, with the potion of the turtle master. But Mason's mind still raced with worry.

As the guardian passed by, Mason slowly turned his head. Behind him, Asher mined quickly, sending block after block tumbling to the tunnel floor.

Will it be quick enough? Mason wondered. *Will we get out before the guardians discover us—or the potion wears off?*

He was answered by a brilliant light flooding the tunnel. He squeezed his eyes shut and opened them again, barely making out the silhouette of his brother, pumping his fist with joy.

Asher had tunneled out. They'd made it!

Mason pivoted and began to swim toward his brother, wishing the potion was gone now so he could move more quickly. But Luna tugged on his shirt, pulling him back. She shook her head and pointed.

Mason looked, expecting to see a guardian. But he saw nothing but turtles.

The turtles. Luna wouldn't leave without them!

Ms. Beacon wouldn't either. The old woman pushed past Mason, back toward the sea cave. As she pulled a handful of sea grass from her robes, his spirits lifted. Ms. Beacon knew how to lure the turtles. She'd done it before.

The first turtle swam around the sea grass, giving Ms. Beacon a wide berth. But the second one dove low, nibbled the grass, and followed Ms. Beacon as she pulled the grass slowly back into the tunnel.

She swam backward, leading the turtle toward the lit opening, where Asher waited. But halfway down the tunnel, the turtle shifted course, as if frightened by Asher. *Or frightened by all of us,* Mason thought. *We need to get out of the way!*

He inched backward into the pool of swimming turtles, wanting to clear the tunnel for them. But as he plunged into deeper water, he felt a commotion behind him. He turned . . .

. . . and came face to face with a guardian.

Its bulbous eye locked on Mason. It thrashed its tail in the water. And then it charged.

Mason tried to duck, but his limbs wouldn't move! All he could do was close his eyes and brace for the guardian's attack. *Please let the potion work,* he prayed, imagining an imaginary shield protecting him from the blast.

He saw a flash of yellow light and then felt the blast knocking him backward against the rock wall. He felt no pain, but for a long terrifying moment, he couldn't move. As Mason clung to the wall, he saw the mob swim away.

It'll be back, Mason knew. He wiggled his fingers and toes, relieved he could still feel them. Then he began to inch his way back toward the tunnel.

The guardian beat him to it. This time, the beast locked its eye on Luna, who turned her head slowly to meet Mason's gaze.

Another flash of light blinded Mason. He squeezed his eyes shut, but not before seeing the laser strike. Had it hit Luna? She would be protected by potion of the turtle master. *But what if it went straight down the tunnel? Toward Asher?*

Panic flooded Mason's chest. He tried to fight his way into the tunnel, but turtles had begun to swim inside. They had found their exit and were swimming to freedom.

Let me in! Mason wanted to cry. Four turtles hurried by, maybe five. Then Luna swam into view, moving more quickly now.

Is the potion wearing off? he wondered. *Yes!* He felt a jolt of energy shoot through his limbs. Then he began to swim, quickly reaching Luna.

He could see the light at the end of the tunnel. Ms. Beacon hovered just beyond it. He could see her rippling robes. But where was Asher?

As Mason broke free from the cave, bursting out into open water, he couldn't find his brother. He looked up, hoping to see Asher swimming toward the surface. Then he looked down, his stomach gripping with fear.

But Asher was gone.

CHAPTER 15

Mason swam in a circle, trying not to panic. Had his brother been struck by the guardian's laser? Had he been hurt or . . . worse?

Mason swam toward Ms. Beacon, hoping for answers. But she was following the turtles now, as if she hadn't even noticed Asher was gone.

Stop! Mason wanted to shout. *What's the matter with you? My brother is more important than those turtles!*

As Luna began to swim after Ms. Beacon, Mason had no choice but to follow. But he didn't fall in line. Instead, he shot past the old woman, determined to get her attention.

Ms. Beacon finally faced him, a smile in her eyes. She pointed straight ahead down the line of turtles. The turtle in the lead seemed to be following something. But what?

Mason swam closer until he could see. A clump of sea grass darted through the water, as if pulled along by an invisible fishing rod.

As he watched the sea grass in wonder, a boy's hand appeared. Then an arm. Then a green T-shirt.

Asher!

Questions darted through Mason's mind, quickly followed by an answer. Asher had used the potion of invisibility—again. But this time, Mason wasn't angry. He'd never been so happy to see his little brother.

As Asher's smiling face appeared, Mason grinned back. They swam together, leading the turtles toward the island—the island where not long ago, those turtles themselves had hatched.

We're leading them home! Mason thought. And this time, he knew they were going to make it. *Finally.*

*   *   *

"When will they hatch?" Asher asked. He lay on his belly in the sand, staring at the pile of precious turtle eggs. Some of the cream-colored shells were larger than the others, but all were speckled with greenish blue flecks.

And all of them hold baby turtles, Mason thought with a smile.

"They could take a week or more to hatch," said Luna as she played with a blade of sea grass. "Right, Ms. Beacon?"

The old woman, who was staring out at the rising sun, nodded.

"A week?" Mason hoped he had heard her wrong.

"We can't stay here that long. Who's going to protect the eggs from the drowned—and other mobs?"

The sea turtles had gone back out to open water, leaving their eggs behind. But those eggs looked so fragile, so vulnerable. Mason scooted closer in the sand.

"Maybe we could use a potion on them," Asher said thoughtfully.

"You mean like potion of invisibility?" Luna cast him a sideways glance.

Asher's cheeks flushed. "No, I used all that up," he admitted. "I'm sorry—I shouldn't have taken it without asking."

Luna nodded. "No, you shouldn't have."

Mason nudged his brother. "You scared me to death back there in the cave," he said. "I thought that you'd fought the guardians—and lost."

"No!" Asher said. "I wasn't fighting. I was trying to save the turtles. I figured if they couldn't see me, they wouldn't be scared, and they would follow me out of the tunnel."

Ms. Beacon reached out and laid a wrinkled hand on his shoulder. "You saved them," she said. "Your older brother taught you well." She shifted her gaze toward Mason and gave him a little nod.

"Me?" Mason shook his head. "No, I didn't have anything to do with . . ."

She raised her hand. "You did," she said. "You taught your brother that there's a time to fight, and a time to turn the other way. You led him, just as he led the turtles."

As the sun cast its first few rays over the beach, Mason felt his own cheeks flush with warmth and pride. But as he turned back toward the eggs, he wondered again, *How will we protect the baby turtles?*

He gazed along the shore, toward the shipwreck he and Asher had once called home. The planks of the hull were weathered and cracked, and the mast bowed downward, nearly touching the ship's rail. As he stared at the ship, a plan formed in Mason's mind.

"I have an idea," he said to Asher. "C'mon!"

* * *

"Is it almost time?" Asher asked again.

Luna sighed. "I told you," she said. "The eggs will hatch any day now. But you can't rush it."

They sat on the beach beside a square pen that Mason and Asher had built with planks from Uncle Bart's ship. Nestled safely inside were the precious turtle eggs.

It had been seven or eight days now—enough time to go home and unpack potion ingredients. Ms. Beacon was busy brewing new potions in her cave. But Mason, Luna, and Asher had come back to watch the baby turtles hatch and lead them safely to water.

"Waiting is hard," Asher said, pushing himself up to his feet. "I'm going to explore Uncle Bart's ship again."

"I'll come too," Mason said, leaping up. "Luna, you'll keep watch, right?"

She nodded, resting her chin on her knees. As the sun set low in the sky, she gazed out over the open water, as if daring the drowned to rise and try to harm those turtle eggs.

The eggs are safe, Mason thought as he followed his brother through the hole in the hull of the ship.

As he poked through the wreckage of boards and mob drops, he remembered a time when he and Asher *hadn't* been so safe. In the days after the shipwreck, they'd had to sleep in this cracked hull. Hostile mobs had crept out of the water onto the beach. Phantoms had swooped overhead.

Mason shivered, shaking off the memory. "Wait up!" he called to Asher, who had already disappeared down the hall toward the bow of the ship. That was where Uncle Bart had kept his supply chest, which had long since been depleted. But there were other chests hidden throughout the ship, too.

Mason found Asher standing in a tiny room lined with fishing gear. Some of the rods had fallen into the cobweb-lined corners of the room. As Mason reached for one, his hand brushed against a sticky web. He pulled back, remembering the spider that had almost taken Asher's life.

"Let's get out of here," he said, checking the ceiling for any furry, red-eyed mobs.

Asher shook his head. "Don't you see those?" He pointed.

"What?" Mason glanced again at the rods on the wall. In the midst of the collection hung a bound bunch of arrows—long, straight, and very sharp.

"There must be a bow around here somewhere," Asher said, scanning the walls.

Mason spotted a weathered chest in a corner and carefully made his way toward it. As he opened the trunk, he found bedding: a red wool blanket that smelled of must. As he pushed it aside, he sucked in his breath.

Beneath the red wool blanket lay another one dyed golden yellow—*sunflower* yellow. "Asher!" Mason cried as he pulled the blanket from the chest.

"I know!" Asher said. "I found it!" But he wasn't looking at the blanket. He was sliding an old wooden bow out from behind a stack of warped planks.

Forgetting the blanket for just a moment, Mason reached for the arrows that hung on the wall. He handed one to Asher, hoping the string on the old bow was strong enough to hold the arrow.

Sure enough, Asher was able to load the arrow and pull back on the string. As he scanned the room, searching for a target, Mason jumped sideways. "Don't point that at me!" he cried. "Let's go outside and try it."

No sooner had he spoken than Mason heard someone cry out. *Luna?* Then he heard a grunt. And a growl.

Dusk had fallen, and brought with it a drowned.

CHAPTER 16

Asher raced from the room. But instead of running back down the hall, he ran up a set of stairs toward the deck of the ship.

"Wait!" Mason cried. He stood at the base of the stairs, still clutching the old yellow blanket.

Asher would be safe up above. But Luna? And the turtles? They were down below, in the sand. Mason ran down the hall, hoping to reach them in time.

As he raced out through the cracked hull, he tossed the old blanket onto the ground and reached for his trident. Even from a distance, he could see Luna was in trouble. She stood in front of the pen surrounding the turtle eggs, but she held no weapon. What had she done with her trident?

Mason spotted the weapon resting against a rock on the beach, way too far away.

The drowned was closing in, staggering through the sand in its tattered brown robes. Mason thought fast, and did the only thing he could do. He raised his trident and threw it with all his might. But the trident missed its mark! It soared over the drowned and landed with a splash in the water.

No! Mason sprinted toward Luna, hoping to reach her in time. But he couldn't move fast enough in the slippery sand.

Then something whizzed through the air overhead. *Thwack!* The drowned dropped backward with a groan.

Mason glanced up just in time to see Asher step back from the deck rail with Uncle Bart's old bow. Then he disappeared. *Yes!* Mason thought, pumping his fist. But he kept running. The drowned was down, but not for long.

By the time Mason reached Luna's side, she had grabbed her own weapon. With a whack of her trident, she finished off the drowned. It left a pile of rotten flesh in its wake.

As Mason kicked sand over the top of the putrid flesh, he glanced over his shoulder, looking for Asher. His brother was hurrying out of the hull, suddenly looking very small with his large wooden bow. Asher's eyebrows were knit together with worry.

"What's wrong?" Mason asked. "Luna's okay, and the eggs are, too."

Asher shrugged. "I didn't count to ten. Maybe I shouldn't have fought. I might have hurt Luna with my arrow."

"No!" said Mason, throwing his arm around Asher's shoulder. "You did well. It's okay to fight to protect something you care about."

Asher's eyes drifted toward the fenced-in pen. "Like the turtle eggs?"

Mason smiled, remembering a time when Asher hadn't cared about the turtles at all—when he had wished they were dolphins instead. "Like the turtle eggs," he repeated.

"And me!" said Luna, elbowing Asher's arm. "You were protecting me too, right?"

He grinned and nodded.

Luna pointed toward the bow in Asher's hands. "Where did you find that?" she asked.

As Asher told her about the weathered old bow, Mason suddenly remembered the blanket he had found. He raced around the ship and gathered the blanket from the ground, shaking off the sand and folding it neatly.

Then he hurried back to the beach and handed it to Asher. "This was yours," Mason said. "Mom dyed it yellow with dye made from sunflowers. Do you remember it now?"

Asher reached for the blanket. He unfolded it and studied the woven pattern. Then he bunched it up and rubbed the soft wool against his cheek. Slowly, he nodded. "I think so," he said, his voice sounding far away.

Mason fought the urge to cheer. He glanced at Luna, and was surprised to see her face fall. She looked as if she'd just lost her best friend.

"What's wrong?" he asked.

She turned away. "You're going back to the sunflower plains someday, aren't you?" she asked. "You and Asher."

When her voice wobbled, Mason suddenly understood. *That's why she was so weird about me going to the sunflower plains,* he realized. *She's afraid Asher and I are going to move away!*

He stepped around Luna so she could see his face. "No," he said. "Our home isn't there anymore. We're staying with you, Luna."

Her eyes flickered upward and met his. She smiled.

Crack!

Luna sucked in her breath and dropped to her knees. She crawled closer to the turtle eggs, peering beneath the wooden slats of the pen. "It's happening," she whispered. "Get over here. It's happening!"

Mason squatted beside her, making room for Asher to squeeze in between. As they fell into silence, Mason heard another *crack*. And then another.

Fine brown lines began to appear on the turtle eggs. Finally, one broke open.

The turtle that crawled out was so tiny! Mason was dying to reach down and scoop it into his hands, but he knew better. "Don't touch it," he whispered to Asher.

"I know that!" said Asher. "Look—another one is hatching!"

Soon, the tiny turtles were roaming out of the pen, searching for water. "Stand back," said Luna. "Let's show them the way."

She pulled sea grass from her pocket, but instead of holding it out to the turtles, she offered it to Mason.

She might as well have handed him golden treasure. He took the sea grass carefully, hoping not to drop a single blade, and then crouched before the turtles. He waved the grass gently, getting their attention. One by one, the tiny turtles began to follow.

"They're so small!" exclaimed Asher. "But I bet their shells are super strong."

"That's right," said Luna. "They're stronger than they look. They'll get where they're going, slowly but surely."

Asher rolled up his yellow blanket and laid it in the sand, creating a wall of safety so that none of the turtles would wander off and get lost.

As the first turtle reached the water, Mason sat back. The turtle wiggled through the wet sand until the tide rolled in, taking the turtle back out with it. "Be free, little buddy," Mason waved goodbye.

"It'll come back," said Asher. "When it's grown up and ready to lay eggs. Then it'll come home."

Mason nodded.

Home. This time, instead of picturing the sunflower plains, he pictured the underwater village where he and Asher lived with Luna. *And Ms. Beacon,* he reminded himself, picturing the warm smile she had given him right here on this beach.

As Asher adjusted his blanket, guiding the turtles along a straight path, Mason imagined how the sunflower-yellow blanket would look spread out on Asher's bed. And he smiled.

We can't go back to our first home, like the turtles do, he decided. *But we can bring a piece of it to our new house.*

As the last turtle reached the water, Mason turned toward Asher.

"It's our turn," he said to his brother. "Let's go home."